AN INVISIBLE BEN STORY

Charlie's New School

ORCHARD BOOKS
96 Leonard Street, London EC2A 4RH
Orchard Books Australia
14 Mars Road, Lane Cove, NSW 2066

ISBN 1 85213 884 X (hardback)
ISBN 1 86039 098 6 (paperback)

First published in Great Britain 1995
First paperback publication 1996
Text © Carmen Harris 1995
Illustrations © Lis Toft 1995

A CIP catalogue record for this book is available
from the British Library.

Printed in Great Britain by Guernsey Press, C.I.

AN INVISIBLE BEN STORY

Charlie's New School

By
Carmen Harris
Illustrated by Lis Toft

ORCHARD BOOKS

CONTENTS

CHAPTER ONE

"Uuhhh!" groaned Charlie for the tenth time, tossing and turning in bed.

Mum and Dad frowned and pursed their lips. What on earth could be the matter?

"Uuhhh!" groaned Charlie again.

His mother put her hand on his forehead.

"He's as hot as a cooked beetroot," she said, pulling it away. "I think it's time to call the doctor."

"No, don't! I'll be all right," groaned Charlie.

"That's what you said the last time," said his father. "It's about time we found out why this bug keeps coming back."

"I'll be all right tomorrow," muttered

7

Charlie bravely.

"Hmmm," breathed Charlie's dad, thoughtfully.

"I'll fetch some aspirins," said Mum, going out of the door.

Dad hovered over the bed and kept saying "Hmmm." Charlie burrowed under the duvet, wishing his father would go away.

He was burning up and wanted to throw off all the covers.

"Hmmm," Dad sighed, resting his chin on his knuckles and staring down at Charlie. Charlie waited and waited, and roasted and roasted. Then it all went quiet. He opened one eye and peeped over the top of the duvet. Then he opened the other eye, raised his head, sat up and flung the duvet to one side.

"Phew!" he gasped, pulling off his pyjama top. He really was hot!

"Hmmm!"

Charlie froze, with his pyjama top still wrapped round his head.

"Charlie?" said Dad, who hadn't left the room at all but was standing by the window.

Charlie just sat there, with his pyjama top half on and half off. Underneath, in the darkness, he opened his eyes wide, wondering what to do next.

"Charlie?" said Dad again, moving towards the bed.

"Charlie!" shouted Mum. She'd come back with the aspirins and a glass of water.

Dad yanked the pyjama top off Charlie's head. Charlie looked pathetically at his mother and father.

"What's the meaning of this?" they both asked, pointing a finger. Beside Charlie lay two very full and very hot hot-water bottles.

CHAPTER TWO

"No more fooling around," warned Charlie's father, giving him a stern look before dashing to open the front door.

"No, Dad," said Charlie, following behind.

"Make sure you get to school and stay there," he said, rushing down the path to open the gate.

"Yes, Dad," said Charlie, glumly stepping on to the path.

"Charlie," called Mum. She stood on the doorstep and tapped one side of her face. Charlie pecked his mother on the cheek and turned to go again.

"Charlie," she called again. "Are you

sure you don't want me to come with you?"

"Yes," he said.

"What about your father? You could run after him."

Charlie watched his father disappear up the road, waving his newspaper to flag down a bus.

"No," he said.

"So, you'll be OK?"

"Yes," said Charlie doubtfully.

"Cheer up, Charlie," said his mother, ruffling his hair. "You'll soon make some friends. This is only your first term at the new school."

"Yes, Mum," said Charlie, and he opened the gate and set off down the road.

Mum watched him go and sighed.

At the bottom of the road Charlie passed the local school. All his friends went there, but it was full up, so Charlie had had to go to another school further away.

"Hi, Charlie," shouted one of Charlie's friends, before rushing into the playground. "You're going to be late."

But there was nothing Charlie could do about his feet taking their own time. With each step, his bag seemed to become heavier and heavier. And each time he thought of his own school, he could feel the soles of his feet turn to toffee and stick to the pavement.

"Hurry up, Charlie," said someone else, running up from behind.

"Hurry up yourself!" said Charlie

grumpily.

"Nice to see you *too*!"

Charlie recognized the voice and turned to see Ben. Ben was the friend who was always getting him into trouble. Charlie hadn't seen him since the last time he had been blamed for doing something Ben had done.

"What are *you* doing here?" Charlie asked crossly.

"You haven't seen me for ages and that's

all you can say?" asked Ben.

"You're not coming to school with me, if that's what you think," said Charlie.

"Oh, go on, I want to see what it's like," said Ben.

"No! Get lost!" said Charlie, in a foul mood.

"Come along, Charlie. School bell's gone," said the lollipop lady, stopping the traffic. She nudged him on the back to hurry him over the crossing.

"Look out for Ben!" cried Charlie,

turning back. Ben had fallen behind and the cars had started to leap across the zebra stripes, heading straight for him.

"Ben? Who's Ben? Where's Ben?" asked the lollipop lady, turning round and twirling her lollipop stick. But she saw no one.

"Ooh, you cheeky little thing, you gave me a fright. Off you go! And I wouldn't play tricks this early in the morning. You'll get yourself into trouble, you will."

Charlie sighed. Either she needed new glasses or she was pretending not to see Ben.

But then, most people didn't seem to notice Ben. Charlie's very own mother and father claimed they never saw Ben — even when he was right there in front of them. "Figment of Charlie's imagination" is what they called him. *Some* figment! Here was Ben walking one step behind Charlie for everyone to see.

"Come on," said Charlie. "If I leave you on your own, you'll only get into trouble."

Ben grinned from ear to ear.

"But make sure you behave and don't get me into trouble!" warned Charlie.

"Sure, Charlie," said Ben, skipping alongside his best friend.

CHAPTER THREE

"Keep still!" hissed Charlie as Ben fidgeted and squirmed beneath his desk.

"I'm bored. My knees hurt," complained Ben. "When can I come out?"

"I *told* you. When class is over," whispered Charlie.

"Shhh!" shushed Mr Hunt, peering over his spectacles and giving Charlie a stern look.

Francine turned round so quickly to sneer at Charlie that her two long plaits swished across Charlie's books and knocked his rocket pencil case off the desk.

"Ouch!" cried Ben as the tip of the rocket spiked him on the head.

"Charlie!" shouted Mr Hunt.

"It wasn't me, Sir," said Charlie.

"You've been whispering and hissing and talking to yourself all lesson. One more disturbance and you're in trouble," warned Mr Hunt.

Francine giggled into her hands. The whole class giggled into their hands.

Charlie's face grew hot with embarrassment, and he had to stop himself kicking Ben for getting him into trouble. But beneath the desk, Ben was busy getting his own back.

"Hands up those who've finished their English homework," said Mr Hunt.

He looked around the class. There wasn't a single hand in the air.

Everyone looked at Charlie. Charlie *always* finished his English. Charlie wanted to put his hand up because he had done his homework, but he didn't dare. Francine would only make fun of him, and then the whole class would join in.

Mr Hunt looked straight at Francine.

"Francine, I expected you to make an extra effort, since your marks for English have been so atrocious this term."

Francine fiddled with her flash new rainbow pen with the four ink colours and pretended not to hear. Anyone getting ticked off was usually worth a laugh, but no one dared to laugh at Francine. Except Ben. But no one heard him quietly chuckling under Charlie's desk.

"Charlie," said Mr Hunt. "I'm sure you've finished your homework. Can I have it please?" There was nothing Charlie could do but pull the sheet of paper from the top of his bag and give it to Sir. Charlie could hear Francine giggling. Goody-goody Charlie, that was what she was thinking. Soon the whole class would be giggling.

"What's the meaning of this, Charlie?" asked Mr Hunt. He waved the sheet of paper

in front of Charlie. Charlie's work was scribbled over and crossed out with circles and lines and squirly squiggles in four different rainbow colours.

"I don't find this very funny," said Mr Hunt, staring at Charlie.

Charlie gulped nervously. Francine roared with laughter and slipped her rainbow pen into her pocket. The whole class roared with laughter.

Mr Hunt turned to face the class. "If your homework isn't in by tomorrow, you will all be staying in for detention — including you, Charlie."

"Yes, Sir!" said Charlie.

"Right. Next lesson, PE," said Mr Hunt.

"Hurray!" shouted the class.

"Whose turn is it to show the rest of the class their movements?" asked Mr Hunt.

Charlie was too miserable to get excited, but the rest of the class shot up their hands.

Francine went one better. She leapt to her feet and waved both her arms in the air like a windmill.

"Me, me, me, Sir!" she cried, then toppled and fell over backwards, taking her chair with her.

First there was silence, then from beneath Charlie's desk came a loud roar of laughter. Everyone looked at Charlie, thinking it was him. Then the whole class bellowed with laughter.

"Stop that!" shouted Mr Hunt. "Francine? Francine, are you all right?"

Francine rose slowly from the floor. The chair rose slowly with her and dangled behind her back. The class broke out into laughter again. They roared and pointed at the sight of Francine's two long plaits tied into two giant knots on the back of the chair. Underneath Charlie's desk, Ben was hopping about on all fours, crying with laughter.

One person who wasn't laughing was Charlie. There were two other people who weren't laughing either — Francine and Mr Hunt. In fact, they were both staring very hard at Charlie.

"Upstairs to the Headmistress!" ordered Mr Hunt.

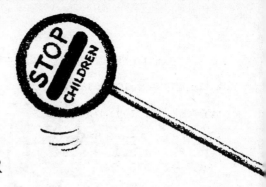

CHAPTER FOUR

Play bell rang and Charlie was still waiting outside the Headmistress's office. End of play bell rang and Charlie was still sitting on the same chair. End of school bell rang and Charlie was beginning to feel he'd be waiting till start of school the next day. Then the Headmistress's door opened and a long, thin finger beckoned Charlie inside. Charlie gulped. As usual, Ben was nowhere to be seen once he'd got Charlie into trouble.

"Now," said Miss Tingle, looking out of the window at the children filling the playground and leaving to go home. "Mr Hunt tells me you've been a nuisance in class today."

"Yes, Miss," said Charlie, looking down and taking great interest in the tips of his shoes. He'd found this was the best way to stop himself being nervous.

"Tying someone's plaits to their chair isn't very clever, is it, Charlie?" asked Miss Tingle.

"No, Miss," said Charlie, noticing that one shoe was actually larger than the other. How come he'd never noticed that before? He shuffled his feet together to compare them. Yes, his left was definitely larger than his right.

"Never mind that she happens to be my niece. The fact is, what you did was a very silly and dangerous thing."

"Yes, Miss," said Charlie, but he wasn't listening. He was too busy wondering if all his other shoes didn't match. He made a note to check when he got home.

"Charlie, have you made any friends at school?" asked Miss Tingle. She waited for a reply. "Charlie?"

Charlie was in a world of his own. He was trying to see whether there was anything interesting about his shoelaces. Maybe one was fatter than the other.

"Charlie!" snapped Miss Tingle.

"Have I... Have I... ?" Charlie stammered, looking up from his shoes.

"Have you made friends with anyone in your class?"

"No, Miss"

"Why not?"

"Because they're scared, Miss. Francine tells everyone not to talk to me — so they don't."

"Francine? My niece? You're saying my niece is being a bully in class?" asked Miss Tingle, showing great interest.

This was the first time Charlie had heard that Francine was Miss Tingle's niece! Now he really *was* in trouble.

"Who, Miss?" he said, trying to think of a way to change the subject.

"Francine," repeated Miss Tingle. "Tell me about the bullying." She moved closer till the light shone on her glasses and Charlie couldn't see her eyes.

"What bullying?" gulped Charlie.

Miss Tingle looked at Charlie, shook her head and sighed. "I think it might be a good idea to ask your parents if they'd like to come and talk about how you're settling in."

"Yes, Miss," said Charlie, breathing a sigh of relief that it was all over.

Outside Ben was waiting. "What took you so long?" he asked.

CHAPTER FIVE

Of course, Charlie didn't say anything to his parents. That would only mean he'd get into trouble all over again. It also meant that for the whole of the next day Charlie had to keep dodging Miss Tingle. All because of Ben — again! Now they were going into the gym to do PE and she was standing by the door, talking to Sir.

"Quick! Behind me," said Ben.

"I thought I told you to stay away," said Charlie.

"You don't want to get into trouble, do you?" asked Ben.

"I *am* in trouble!" growled Charlie.

But they were getting closer to Miss

Tingle, so Charlie did as Ben said and hid behind him as the class moved towards the door of the gym.

"Don't *push*!" huffed Francine, turning round.

"It's not me, it's Ben," whispered Charlie, keeping his head down and shuffling up against Ben, who was shuffling up against Francine.

"If you don't stop," shouted Francine, "I'll tell my aunty —— I mean, Miss Tingle."

"What's happening over there?" asked Miss Tingle.

At that moment Ben grabbed Charlie by the arm. They ducked and made a dash past Francine, right under Miss Tingle's nose, around Mr Hunt and through the double doors into the gym.

"Find a partner and practise what we started last week," Mr Hunt shouted into the hall. "We'll be having wet play in there, so put your lunch boxes in the corner. I'll be with you as soon as I've finished my conversation with Miss Tingle."

The class piled their bags in a corner and started looking for partners. Charlie hated PE. No one ever wanted to be his partner. And even if someone did, Francine would start picking on them until they found another partner. Charlie stood in the corner beside the bags and watched as the class paired up. Francine turned and smiled sweetly at Charlie, then stuck her tongue out at him.

"Never mind," said Ben, poking his head out from behind the horse. "I'll be your partner."

"Don't be stupid," said Charlie. "You don't even go to this school."

"What do you think I'm *doing* here?" he asked. "And anyway, *someone's* got to show that Francine she's not the best at PE, haven't they?"

Charlie wasn't sure. No matter what it was, whenever he and Ben did anything together he was always the one who got into trouble. But Ben had already made up his mind and was standing beside Charlie.

"Just watch her face!" he said. "Lie down on your back and toss me in the air with your feet, like I'm a rubber ball."

"I can't do that!" said Charlie.

"Trust me," said Ben. "You can do it."

So Charlie tried it. And it worked! Ben curled into a ball and Charlie pumped his

legs up and down till Ben was spinning and rolling and bouncing on the end of his feet like a circus seal. It was amazing! It was so amazing, the whole class stood in a huddle and watched. At last! At last! thought Charlie. Now he'd show the class that he *could* do things, that he wasn't just silly old Charlie, that he . . .

"Look at that wally!" laughed Francine.
"What does he think he is? Are we supposed
to be impressed? Oh, someone be his partner
quick before his skinny legs fall off!"

And, of course, the whole class started to laugh at Charlie trying his best without a partner.

Charlie was just about to say, "I have got a partner! Can't you see?" when he realized that Ben had rolled off and was lying beside the bags. Charlie stopped pumping his legs.

"What are you doing?" he asked. "You're supposed to be my partner."

"I got thirsty," replied Ben, taking a carton of blackcurrant juice out of Charlie's bag and punching it with a straw. "Oops!"

Charlie watched as a stream of black juice squirted from the straw, sprayed over his head and whooshed across the gym where it landed in a big bluey-black splodge on Francine's clean white PE top. She stopped laughing. The whole class stopped laughing. Francine looked down at her shirt.

When she looked up, Charlie was holding the carton of blackcurrant juice Ben had just put in his hand.

"Right!" said Francine. Then she stomped over to grab her bag. "Come on, you lot!" she shouted. "This is war!"

Before Charlie knew what was happening, he was under attack. Squirts of orange juice, raspberry juice, apple juice and Frankenstein juice, and frothy streams of shaken-up fizzy cola, cream soda and bubble-gum soda showered the air and fell on him till he was drenched in seven different sticky colours. Then juice started flying in all directions. Screams and shouts

43

and cheers filled the hall as everyone chucked and squirted juice, skidded on puddles of juice and raided other people's bags for more juice. It seemed to go on for ever before the doors flew open and Mr Hunt's big voice filled the hall: "Who started this?"

CHAPTER SIX

"You wait! You just wait!" Francine kept muttering.

Charlie took no notice. He was on to his sixth sheet of paper and was furiously scribbling away. Mr Hunt had made them miss PE to write twenty reasons why fighting in class is not allowed. Charlie only had to think of another three before he was finished.

"I know one! I know one!" said Ben for the fifth time.

Charlie was trying to ignore him, but now he had had enough. Enough of his big mouth and enough of his interfering.

"Shut up!" Charlie shouted.

"Don't tell me to shut up," shouted

Francine from across the room.

"I wasn't. I was talking to Ben," said Charlie.

"Oh, very funny," said Francine.

"Why won't you let me help you?" asked Ben.

"Because you get on my nerves. Because you always get me into trouble. Because I don't want you hanging around me — so get lost!" shouted Charlie angrily.

"Fine!" said Ben in a sulk. "I'm going!"

"What did you say?" asked Francine.

"Good!" said Charlie as Ben walked out of the door.

"Good, what?" asked Francine.

"I wasn't talking to you," said Charlie, relieved that Ben had now gone.

"Don't think I don't know what you're up to!" said Francine.

Just then Mr Hunt came into the room. "I hope you've both been working and not mucking about," he said.

"Sir, my aunty will be very cross if she knows I've missed PE," said Francine.

"Your aunty will be extremely cross if she finds out *why* you've missed PE," said Mr Hunt, picking up Francine's single sheet of paper. He looked at the blotches and scribbles and crossed-out lines and he frowned.

"I can't *think*," whined Francine.

"Twenty's too hard, Sir. Can't we do five?"

"How about *one*, Francine?" Mr Hunt asked, turning the paper on to the other side. "Start again."

"Aw, *Sir!*" she wailed. "I'm no good at English."

"Use your imagination," said Mr Hunt.

"I don't have one," cried Francine, "I'm only good at PE."

"Finished!" Charlie waved his papers in the air triumphantly.

Francine gave him a terrible look.

"You wait!" she hissed.

CHAPTER SEVEN

Charlie didn't have long to wait. After school, he took the long way home through the park and Francine jumped on him from a chestnut tree. Or at least, she tried to. Charlie heard a *"Crack!"* and someone shouting above his head,

"I'm going to flatten you, Charlie Fraser."

He looked up and saw a blur in the sky, then something big bobbing up and down between the trees.

"Ow! I'm stuck!" yelled Francine.

There she was dangling in the air like a rag doll, her two big plaits caught in the branches.

"Help me! Help me!" she cried.

"Why should I?" asked Charlie. "You were going to jump on me."

"If you don't help me, I'll *get* you!" yelled Francine. She kicked both legs and swung on the branches, which sent her spinning round and round in midair.

Charlie just carried on walking. But halfway up the road he began to think. What would Miss Tingle say if Francine told her he'd seen her stuck up a tree and went home to have his tea instead of helping her? What if *he* was ever stuck up a tree? He'd be very annoyed if he shouted to someone and they just walked past and ignored him. Charlie let out a big sigh. He wasn't happy about it, but he supposed he ought to help. Just as Charlie was about to turn and walk back, Ben appeared.

"Don't go," he said. "It's a trick."

"I've got to go," said Charlie. "Suppose it isn't a trick. I'll only get into trouble."

So Charlie turned and walked back to the tree, and Ben followed.

But when he got there the tree was empty.

Charlie was very annoyed with himself. It was all a trick. Francine was only pretending to be stuck — and he had fallen for it. She was probably hiding in the bushes right now and laughing at him.

"Told you," said Ben.

Charlie and Ben turned and started to head for home. Then they heard a noise. A very loud rattling noise. It was coming from inside the can bank beneath the chestnut tree. He noticed a big tin lid propped against the side which the can-bank men had forgotten to put back. Then he heard a hollow voice.

"Charlie! Charlie! Help me out." It was Francine.

"Where are *you*?" asked Charlie, still not sure whether this was all part of the prank.

Rattle! Rattle!

"Where do you think?" boomed Francine's echo. "I fell into the can bank!"

"How am I supposed to get you out?" asked Charlie.

"How do *I* know? Use your imagination!" yelled Francine.

Rattle! Rattle!

"I'll run back to school and get Miss Tingle," said Charlie.

Then he heard something he'd never heard before: Francine crying.

"Boo-hoo, boo-hoo!" she sobbed. "Don't tell my aunty! I'll get into trouble. Don't leave me! It's dark and stinky in here."

Rattle! Rattle!

But what could Charlie do? If he climbed on top of the can bank, he'd never be able to reach her inside. Besides, he'd probably fall in too. Then he remembered something.

"I won't be long!" shouted Charlie.

"Boo-hoo! Boo-hoo!" Rattle! Rattle! was all Charlie could hear.

"Don't cry," said Charlie. "Ben will stay with you."

"Who's Ben?" echoed Francine. "Not that trick you were playing in the classroom?"

"He's not a trick. He's here with me."

Charlie turned to Ben. "Say something, Ben."

"Hello," said Ben.

But Francine kept quiet. She didn't believe a word of it.

"See you in a minute," said Charlie, running off and leaving Ben beside the can bank.

Ben pressed his ear against the metal sides. "Hello," he said again. But all he could hear inside was *Rattle! Rattle! Rattle!*

CHAPTER EIGHT

Charlie ran as fast as he could. On and on, till he got to the place in the park where there was a sort of brick box with a wooden door. This was where the park keepers put all the dead leaves when they swept the park. It was also where the lollipop lady hid her lollipop stick. He opened the wooden door and pulled out the long pole. "I'll help her all by myself!"

When Charlie ran back towards the tree, he could see Ben stooping beside the can bank.

"Here he comes," Ben said to Francine.

"Here I am," said Charlie.

"What took you so long?" askedFrancine.

Charlie climbed up the tree and stepped on to the top of the can bank as Ben passed him the lollipop stick. He stood on the edge and looked down inside the gloomy darkness. Francine wobbled and stumbled on top of an enormous pile of tin cans. *Rattle!*

Rattle! She looked up to the light as Charlie dangled the stick end of the lollipop in the air above her head.

"Hold on," said Charlie.

"I can't! I can't!" Francine whimpered. "You'll let go and I'll fall again and hurt myself even more."

"Course I won't," boomed Charlie's voice around the insides of the can bank.

"I've got Ben to help me."

"Stop fooling around," cried Francine. "Ben's only pretend."

"You were just talking to him," said Charlie.

"So what? He's still only pretend," sobbed Francine.

Then Ben poked his head over the top of the can bank. "Here I am," he said.

"There he is," said Charlie.

Francine looked up and squinted. She couldn't see anything apart from Charlie's head bobbing against the sky. She was cut and bruised and miserable, and she really wanted to get out. But Charlie wasn't strong enough to pull her out all by himself. She squinted again. This time she saw two faces peering down at her from the opening.

"You won't let me fall?" she asked.

"Course not," yelled Ben. "I'm stronger than him."

So Francine gripped the pole, and Charlie and Ben gripped the round end of the lollipop. While they heaved and pulled, Francine used her strong legs against the sides of the can bank as though she was climbing the ropes in the school gym. Bit by bit, she inched towards the top. Bit by bit, Charlie and Ben grunted and pulled till they got to the end of the pole and Francine's tangly hair and red face appeared in front of them.

"See. We didn't let you fall, did we?" beamed Charlie.

"Thanks, Ben," said Francine, clambering on to the top.

* * * *

"This is the best piece of work I've seen this term," said Mr Hunt, pointing to the essay he had just pinned on the display board. The class filed past to have a look at "The Day Ben Rescued Me from the Can Bank."

"You've written a very exciting essay," continued Mr Hunt. "Your aunt . . . er, Miss Tingle will be very proud of you."

Francine stood beside her new friend, Charlie, and beamed from ear to ear.

Mr Hunt turned to Charlie. "Don't you think she's very imaginative, coming up with a story about this friend who no one else can see?"

Francine and Charlie snorted into their hands at the sight of Ben cheekily popping up from behind Mr Hunt.

"What's so funny?" asked Mr Hunt.

"Nothing, Sir," giggled Charlie and Francine together. "We were just imagining something."

Other brilliant Orchard Books are:

THE MOVING MYSTERY
An Invisible Ben Story
ISBN 1 85213 883 1 Hb

THE SCRIBBLERS OF SCUMBAGG
SCHOOL
Wes Magee
ISBN 1 85213 486 0 Hb
ISBN 1 85213 510 7 Pb

THE WITCH WHO COULDN'T SPELL
Jonathan Allen
ISBN 1 85213 887 4 Hb

TEACHER'S PET
Philip Wooderson
ISBN 1 85213 780 0 Hb